T0380762

Footprints in the Snow

by Kim Ward Storch

To order additional copies of this book, contact:
Xlibris
1-888-795-4274
www.Xlibris.com
Orders@Xlibris.com

Footprints in the Snow

This book is dedicated in loving memory of my dad, Drew Ward.

He was an inspiration. When he put his mind to something it got done.

He started the St. Joseph's Food Cellar feeding the hungry & homeless.

He was an Angel for so many. I feel he is my Angel in Heaven helping me find my words.

Thank you Dad. I love you.

My name is not important…my story is.

I sat alone that day.

Ashamed. Feeling lost. Desperate and scared.

No job. How will I support my family?

I asked myself, "What could I do?"

I thought walking away was the answer.

Tonight is Christmas Eve.

The chill in the cold night air sends a shiver through my spine.

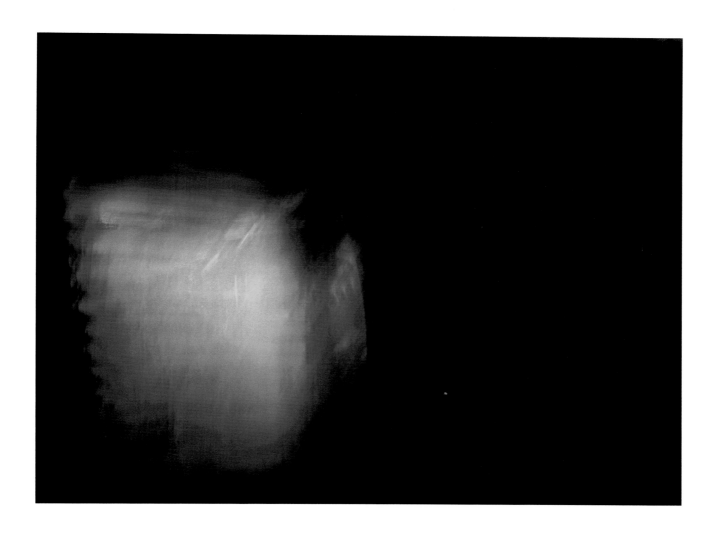

The five of us huddle around the fire trying to keep warm.

Ben and Sara shiver as they hold each other in an embrace.

Jacob throws another log on the fire, making the flames burst a bright glow.

While Stanley clears his throat and speaks.

I stand and listen.

"Max was a handsome boy." Stanley says with a toothless grin.

"Big, fluffy tail…such a good ole' dog."

Taking a sip from the crinkled, brown bag that he always keeps tucked inside his jacket, I watch as he uses the back of his hand to wipe away the burn of alcohol from his chapped lips, as he continues.

"Molly was the pistol…loved to chew my shoes."

"Every Christmas I'd get them the biggest bones I could find…it was the worst day of my life when I had to give 'em away." "Got too expensive to feed 'em."

Stanley tosses the empty bottle in the fire. The five of us watch as the bag burns.

I look over and notice Jacob shifting uncomfortably from one foot to another, when he starts speaking.

"My holidays were always spent at my younger brother's house." He says in disgust.

"My niece and nephew and me would stay up real late playing board games... then one year I just never showed up."

Shrugging he rubs his hands together over the fire.

Under his breath he mumbles, "you always hurt the ones you love."

Quietly Sara speaks, "Ben and I got married last spring and neither of us can find jobs." Ben pulls Sara close, wrapping her in a wool blanket.

"We'd always spend Christmas with friends. Singing Christmas carols and eating gingerbread cookies," Sara says.

I see Sara and Ben smile at the memory.

Looking down at his boots, Ben angrily states, "Never did we imagine this could happen to us."

Sara sniffs as tears swell in her eyes.

We all quietly stand, watching the reds and orange colors flicker in the wind…
getting lost in our own thoughts. The only sound coming from the crackling fire.

The silence between us grows hard and cold like the winter's night. I look around at my four friends, my new family. I think about the past year and how much I ache for my family that I left. So much sorrow. So much hurt.

From out of the darkness, Sara begins a low hum of *Silent Night.* Stanley, Ben and I join her. Jacob stands with his arms folded tightly across his body, scowling as he stares at the fire.

The silence between us grows hard and cold like the winter's night. I look around at my four friends, my new family. I think about the past year and how much I ache for my family that I left. So much sorrow. So much hurt.

Placing my hands deep within my pockets, I decide to take a walk.

Fresh snow begins to fall, covering my path.

As I walked down different streets, I peek into homes. Families are gathered around Christmas trees, laughing and singing. Children are running from room to room with the excitement of Santa's arrival.

It is a joyous time for most...I am filled with sorrow and regret.

Taking a deep breath the cold air burns my lungs. My eyes sting. Is it from the tears that I need so badly to shed or just from the winter's night?

It makes it hard to see.

It is here that I stop. I look at the house in front of me and realize I have walked home. Not much has changed since I left. The holly bush that we planted as a family years before had grown some and the lilacs that lined the street were filling in. I can imagine them this spring. Their fragrant flowers smelling the neighborhood.

I move closer to see the inside; my heart stops as I see them. My son, much taller now, almost a man. My little girl, how beautiful she has become. And there placing the star high upon the tree is my wife. Smiling her radiant smile.

I want to knock at the door but I am frozen. Not from the cold but from fear.

Sighing, I pull my hat down over my ears and walk on whispering a prayer.

A tear drop falls and freezes on my cheeks.

Bending my body forward I try to shield my face from the wind and snow. My eyes are clouded now with tears. I can't see in front of me so I don't notice a branch sticking out of the fresh fallen snow. My boot gets tangled up in its branches as I fall. Banging the cold wet snow in anger, I try to get up.

When suddenly I feel a warm, gentle hand embrace my arm. I glance upward, a soft light shimmers a pale yellow. It all feels calm and so am I.

"What is this?" I wonder.

A voice is heard, "You know what you need to do."

"You have taken the first steps tonight."

"Your journey home has begun."

Suddenly the light is gone but the words spoken open my heart.

A soft glimmer catches my eye and I realize where the light had been a radiant star sits. I pick it up and place it in my pocket.

Looking down, I see that I tripped over a discarded Christmas tree.

Swinging it over my shoulder, I begin my walk back, to Ben and Sara, Jacob and Stanley.

Approaching the fire the flames flicker in the dark. Before it goes out for the night I add more logs. I put the tree in a corner of our little spot my friends and I call home. Remembering the star in my pocket I reach in and place it on top of the tree. I smile.

Stepping back I briefly glance at my friends and whisper to each of them.

"Merry Christmas."

"Peace, God Bless."

Shoving my hands back into my pockets I turn to look at the star. The radiant glow fills my heart with warmth.

I know where I must go.

A very special thank you to…my dear friend Robin. Your friendship and support during this project was the hand I needed to guide me.

Carole for your love and support. You pushed me to get it done. Thank you.

Mom and Denise a big high five for suggesting I use my photographs…who knew?

Derek for your insight. You helped me with the missing piece. And for your comma magic. Thank you. Thank you. Thank you.

To Kurt, Konrad and Koby for your love…

I love you all so much.